"Can you keep a secret?" I ask.

Daniel nods. "I know many secrets."

"My aunt Lily has a dog assistant who helps with her writing," I say.

"Great. I'm not surprised. I told you dogs are smart."

PATRICIA MacLACHLAN

WONDROUS REX

Illustrations by
EMILIA DZIUBAK

KATHERINE TEGEN BOOKS
An Imprint of HarperCollins Publishers

Katherine Tegen Books is an imprint of HarperCollins Publishers.

Wondrous Rex
Text copyright © 2020 by Patricia MacLachlan
Illustrations copyright © 2020 by Emilia Dziubak
All rights reserved. Printed in the United States of America.
No part of this book may be used or reproduced in any manner
whatsoever without written permission except in the case of brief
quotations embodied in critical articles and reviews. For information
address HarperCollins Children's Books, a division of HarperCollins
Publishers, 195 Broadway, New York, NY 10007.
www.harpercollinschildrens.com

Library of Congress Control Number: 2019944596
ISBN 978-0-06-294099-5

Typography by Amy Ryan
21 22 23 24   PC/BRR   10 9 8 7 6 5 4 3 2 1
❖
First paperback edition, 2021

This is for Anna MacLachlan,
a wondrous storyteller.
With love,
P. M.

We can find magic in the sunrise,
the full moon, a kindness,
someone's laughter, and
even in a dog who doesn't talk.

1.

FLUMMOXED

I am seven years old, and my life is soon to be full of "wondrous" happenings. "Wondrous" is a word I learned from my aunt Lily, a writer of books.

Lily lives next door to me, and I go there after school while my mother and father are at work. They are pediatricians, doctors for children. My friend Daniel calls us the "doctor/doctor family."

My parents deal with tonsils, broken bones, blood, and children who throw up on them.

My aunt Lily deals with words. She loves words most of the time, and she has taught me many words, such as "melancholy," "delirious," and, of course, "wondrous."

My teacher, Ms. Luce, is often impressed, but not *too* impressed.

"You know fine words, Grace," she says. "Now why don't you weave them into a story?"

She hands me a journal of empty pages. My name, Grace, is on the cover.

"I don't know how to write a story," I say.

"Only my aunt knows how."

Ms. Luce smiles. "I know you better than you think," she says. "You have stories inside you. You'll find a story or a poem to share one day."

When I let myself into Lily's house she has baked thirty-six frosted ginger cookies and laid them out in rows, and she is eating dill pickles out of a glass jar. Lily always bakes and eats dill pickles when her writing is not going well.

"I'm flummoxed, Gracie," she says.

Another word.

"I don't know what new story to write. I'm like a sailboat without a sail. I'm wandering. I need help. Flummoxed!"

She eats another pickle.

"You will think of something," I say.

"I have put up a notice in the post office, on a grocery bulletin board, and also online for an assistant," Lily said. "Help yourself to a cookie."

She shows me the printed notice.

A WRITER OF BOOKS NEEDS
AN ASSISTANT, A COACH,
A HELPER, FOR INSPIRATION
AND SOME MAGIC!

Lily's email address and contact information are written below the notice.

"An assistant?" I ask.

"Well, a coach, maybe—to help me write."

I see that her desk is a mess of papers and two coffee cups and books. One book is a writers' help book titled *What Now?!*

"Maybe your writers' group will help," I say.

Lily shakes her head. "Maybe. But this

has to come from me. In some new way."

She sighs. "I want magic," she says.

Later Lily and I will remember her word "magic." It turns out to be the very word she gets.

Magic.

2.

THE "L'S"

It is a half day at school, and Lily's writers' group is coming over to her house afterward. I love it when they come. They don't ask me to sit in the group—I might learn their secrets.

Lily puts me at the dining-room table, behind glass doors, closed a bit.

But I am seven years old, don't forget, and I have sharp hearing. I call the group the "L's" because all their names begin with the letter "L": Laura, Lois, Lila, Lacy, Lou, Lana, and my aunt Lily. They write novels for adults and for children, essays, and poetry.

They eat snacks and talk about their news before they read their work aloud. Sometimes I take notes or draw pictures of them. Sometimes their news is "very dramatic," as Lily puts it.

Lily loves my drawings, and she frames them. One says "Sold" and has bright stars all around. The other says "Rejected" and has gray teardrops.

The news today is this:

"My editor did not want my book," says Laura.

"I spoke at a conference last week, and my day job is troublesome. No writing," says Lois.

"It's spring. I work in my garden instead of writing," says Lila. She crosses her legs and bounces one leg up and down. She wants to go back to her garden.

"I sold three picture books. Sent out another," says Lacy.

"I have poems to read today," says Lou.

"I was too tired to write," says Lana,

yawning. "But I have some ideas."

I draw pictures of all the L's in various states of gloom and glee; words I like.

"Are you going to tell the L's that you want an assistant?" I ask when the L's have left.

"No," says Lily, checking her email on her computer.

She sits up quickly. "Oh no! There's an assistant coming soon! Hand me the pickles, please."

"Should I be here?" I ask.

There's a sudden knock at the door.

"Stay," says Lily. "Stay," she repeats.

She takes a deep breath. She opens the door. . . .

3.

REX

A man wearing a tall hat stands there.

He has a brown, smooth-coated dog with a
long tail.

"I have brought you magic," says the man.
"The magic you want."

"Magic?" asks Lily. "I did write that, didn't I?"

"You did. I brought you Rex," he says.

Rex wags his large tail.

The man hands a card to Lily. Lily hands it to me.

The card reads, *Maxwell the Magician*.

"I have never met a magician before," says Lily.

"My pleasure then," says Maxwell, bowing.

"This is Grace," says Lily.

"I bow to Grace," says Maxwell.

And he does.

Rex leans against me. He is heavy and friendly. I slip him a piece of cookie.

"Rex has worked with me for a long time,"

says Maxwell. "But now he's bored. Jake the vet says he's sad. He needs new work. He loves work. He can be your assistant."

"What does Rex do?" asks Lily.

"Most everything you need," says Maxwell. "It will make him happy. It will make you happy."

He puts a bag of dog food and two bowls on the floor. He brings in a soft dog bed from outside the door.

"Let me know how it goes," he says to Lily. "I'll visit if I can."

"Of course," says Lily.

Maxwell leans down to kiss Rex on the head. Then he is gone.

I offer Rex another cookie piece and he eats it.

"Well, I have an assistant," says Lily.

"I can't believe it," I say.

"I can," says Lily. "I'm a writer. I believe most anything."

Rex walks over to Lily's desk. He pushes her scattered papers together in a neat pile with his nose. He carefully picks up the papers on the floor with his teeth. He pushes a chair next to Lily and sits there.

Lily sits down at her computer. She offers Rex a cookie, but he just stares at her with a look that says, "No more cookies. Time for work."

Rex presses the search button on the computer, and his paws move over the keys. A quote appears on the screen.

If you find a book you really want to read but it hasn't been written yet, then you must write it.

—Toni Morrison

Lily reads it.

I read it. I feel goose bumps on my arms.

Lily smiles, her first smile of the day. She begins to write.

And I have a startling thought. An unbelievable thought.

Rex can read!!

Rex reaches over with a paw and magically inserts a comma on Lily's page, then a semicolon.

Lily writes and writes. After a minute she turns and reaches over to stroke Rex's muzzle.

Only once does Rex jump down from his chair. He goes to the door and looks at me. I open the door, and we go out together. We can hear the steady keyboard sounds inside.

Rex goes behind a tree and lifts his leg. And then we go inside; Lily is still writing.

Rex goes over to his dog bed, turns around once, and lies down. He sleeps.

Maxwell the magician was right!

Rex is happy.

Lily is smiling.

She is happy.

4.

MESSAGES

The doctors are home with Chinese food for dinner. Vegetarian for my mother. Garlic chicken for my father. Spicy, amazing orange beef for me.

"So how is Lily?" asks my father.

"She has a new assistant," I say.

"Really?" says my mother, her fork suspended over her plate. Her dinner looks like leaves and twigs. "That's hard to believe," she says.

I think about Lily saying, "I'm a writer. I believe most anything."

"Is she helpful?" asks my father.

"He," I correct him. "*He* is helpful. And he doesn't talk."

"What? How can he help?" My father stares at me.

I smile at what my parents do not yet know.

"It's kind of magical," I say.

My mother and father stare at me for a moment.

Everyone eats.

And once again I get goose bumps on

my arms when I open my fortune cookie. I straighten the paper with the written message.

It reads:

Your talents will soon be recognized.

At school, I show my fortune to Ms. Luce.

"Ah, a message to you!" she says as if she expected it all along—as happy as if the message might have been written by her.

Daniel and I walk home together, talking about his white dog, who guards and herds his farmer grandfather's large flock of sheep.

"Sometimes she walks over their sheep's backs to get to the other side, watching for coyotes or wolves," he says. "Dogs are smart."

"And they don't talk," I say before I know I'm saying it.

"No, they don't," says Daniel matter-of-factly.

I stop walking.

Daniel stops.

"Can you keep a secret?" I ask.

Daniel nods. "I know many secrets."

"My aunt Lily has a dog assistant who helps with her writing," I say.

"Great. I'm not surprised. I told you dogs are smart."

He starts walking again, and I am relieved to have told the secret and to have told it to Daniel.

"What do Doctor and Doctor think about that?" asks Daniel.

"They don't know yet," I say.

Daniel grins his big grin, which means he is truly amused. He doesn't ask any more questions.

"You should write a story about this," says Daniel.

"I don't write stories," I say.

"Soon, maybe," says Daniel as he turns down the road to his grandfather's farm.

He doesn't look back at me.

At Lily's house there are no cookies laid out in neat rows.

There is no dill pickle jar.

There is just the clicking of Lily's keyboard keys as she writes.

Rex is sleeping in his bed, his work over for now. He doesn't hear me come in.

I stand and watch the two of them. I don't want to disturb Lily or wake Rex. But Lily sees me and beckons me over.

"Look what Rex found on the computer," she whispers. "Look!"

I look at the computer screen.

There is a quote.

I write to find out what I think, what I feel,

and what it means; what I want and what
I fear.
　　—P. M.

"A message," I say softly.

I take the fortune cookie paper out of my pocket. Lily reads it. She smiles.

"We're both getting messages," says Lily. "And maybe it's our job to pay attention to them." She grins, a bit like Daniel.

Rex gets up at the sound of Lily's voice, stretches, and comes over to me.

Rex shakes his head toward the door.

He wants out.

Messages.

5.

THE SECRET

My mother and father, Doctor and Doctor, visit Lily after work. I was wondering how long it would take them.

My father kisses Lily.

"My favorite sister," he says.

"Your only sister," says Lily.

"Hi, Gracie, my favorite daughter."

"And only," I say.

Rex goes up to my mother and sits in front of her.

"Hello there," she says, stroking Rex.

"Why do you have this dog?" asks my father, patting Rex.

"His name is Rex," says Lily. "I'm keeping Rex for a friend. He's good company. He relaxes me, and his kindness is inspiring."

I steal a look at Lily. She doesn't look at me.

Lily's not about to tell my mother and father that Rex can use the computer and can read.

"Nice," says my father. "And where's your assistant?"

"Not working with me today," says Lily in a light voice.

Rex looks at my father and mother. He doesn't go to the computer. He doesn't arrange papers. He doesn't sit on the chair by Lily. He shakes his head toward the door.

"He wants out!" says my father. "Smart dog! It's almost like he's talking."

My father goes to the door and looks at Lily. "Does he need a leash?" he asks.

Lily and I laugh.

"Not Rex," I say.

"Not Rex," echoes Lily.

☆☆

Both my parents' phones ring. They listen, then end the calls. "We have to go back to the hospital," says my mother to Lily and me. "Emergency. Four children and a bicycle accident."

Lily waves at them.

"Go, go. Grace can sleep here if you're late. There's no school tomorrow."

My parents kiss me goodbye. They both pat Rex before they go.

"Nice dog," says my father as he goes out the door. "And smart!"

"Rex was a 'regular' dog with my mother and father," I say. "Not your assistant. Did you notice?"

"I did. Rex knows things," says Lily.

Rex looks at us for a moment. He goes to the computer and presses a key.

He moves his paws over the keys. He's very quick.

Lily and I look at each other.

We've never seen him move this fast before.

Two sentences appear on the computer screen.

They are:

Dogs know secrets. Dogs keep secrets.

"Is that a quote from someone?" I ask.

Lily looks like she might cry.

"No," she says slowly. "He wrote it."

She peers at me.

She takes a deep breath.

"It is Rex's message to us," she says. "Rex can write."

"Yes, he can type words," I say.

Lily shakes her head.

"No, Grace. I mean he knows how to tell us his thoughts," says Lily.

Rex jumps down and drinks water from his water bowl. He pushes his food bowl, and Lily pours food into his bowl.

"Rex writes," she says softly. The only sound in the room is Rex crunching his dinner.

When he's done he looks at Lily, then at me.

He knows what we're thinking.

Rex writes.

My mother calls Lily. Lily turns on the speakerphone so I can hear.

"Lots of scrapes and broken bones," she says. "And lots of parents," she adds, making Lily laugh.

"Good night, Grace," says my mother.

"Good night."

I sleep in Lily's guest room. My framed drawings of the writers' group hang on the wall—"Sold" and "Rejected."

In the middle of the night I feel Rex jump up on the bed beside me. He lies down and puts a large front leg over me.

Like a hug.

I look into his face. "You're a writer, Rex," I whisper in the moonlight. "I wish I could be a writer, too."

Rex looks closely at me until my eyes close.

The next morning I wake in sunlight and Rex is gone.

At the bottom of my bed is my empty journal with my name on it.

It is opened to the first page. There is a pen beside it.

I pick it up. Maybe Lily put it there for me. I go to the desk by the window. And I write:

I am seven years old and am writing this for the first time ever. I know words, but I don't yet know how to string them together to shape how I feel and what I think into a story.

But I have help.

And maybe that help will be part of what I write—

Grace

6.

A BIT OF MAGIC

Lily is writing at her computer, her desk neat. The front door is open. I hear Rex woof outside.

Maxwell the magician looks inside, Rex with him.

"Maxwell!" Lily says, smiling. "Come in."

"Hello, Grace," he says to me.

"Hello," I say. "Rex can write!" I blurt out before I know it.

Maxwell sighs.

"Yes, I know," he says. "I didn't tell you. I wanted you to discover his bit of magic yourselves."

Lily smiles at the words "his bit of magic."

"Rex looks so happy," Maxwell says almost wistfully. "Don't worry. I just came for a visit. He's working. Right?"

Lily puts her arms around Maxwell. "He's working!" she says. "I'm working! And I owe you a great deal for him."

Maxwell shakes his head and smiles. "No, I owe *you*. Seeing him happy—seeing you happy—is what I want. He is your dog now."

He hands Lily a card.

"Here's the name of his vet. It's just down the street."

Maxwell bows to us.

"I'll visit from time to time," he says. "I have to go train my chicken."

"A chicken?" I ask.

"A smart chicken," says Maxwell.

"What does the chicken do?"

"I'll let you know the next time I visit."

He kisses Rex on the head.

When he leaves, Rex watches for a moment, then jumps up on his chair.

Lily laughs.

"Okay, okay," she says, sitting beside him.

"Lily, did you put my journal on my bed last night?"

"What journal? No. I did see Rex with his nose in your school backpack," she says.

I look at Rex.

"It was open to page one and there was a pen next to it," I say.

Lily smiles.

"Your father said it—'smart dog.'"

"Little does he know!" I say.

Lily bursts into laughter.

Rex looks over and pushes the search button. His paws move over the keys.

Two quotes appear:

There is joy in work.

Dance like no one is watching.

Lily gets up, grabs my hands, and, without music, we dance wildly around the room, whirling and laughing until we collapse on her couch.

Rex watches us for a moment, then leans over to press a button. Lily's new story comes up.

Winter will soon sit outside with its early dark.

"What are you writing?" I ask.
Lily shakes her head.

"I don't know yet. I'm setting a scene—a time of year. I'll follow it to see where it goes. Winter coming? Is it fearful or *exciting*?"

She smiles at me.

"Maybe Rex will know," she says.

I think of Maxwell's words—

"A bit of magic."

7.

LOVE AND LEMON CAKE

My parents have gone to a medical conference—infant to preteen. It is spring vacation, so I spend my week with Lily and Rex and the L's.

Rex becomes a "regular" dog again when the writers' group meets. He is allowed in the group room while I draw and take notes at the dining-room table, behind glass doors.

They do not know Rex will listen and understand their words.

After a while he pushes the doors open to drink water in the kitchen. He lies under the dining-room table, at my feet.

My journal sits under my notes. I listen with my stocking feet on Rex's body as if he's a footstool.

This is the news:

Every L has something to read this week. No backaches, no gardening, no interruptions in their writing lives. No complaints.

They are eating sweet snacks, so there is a lot of energetic talk.

Rex gets up and shakes his head at the door.

I let him out and see Daniel walking by. He comes over, and we sit on the steps together.

Rex wags his tail.

"Hi, Rex," says Daniel. "I'm Daniel, and you're smart."

Rex sits and offers Daniel a paw.

"He's never done that before," I say.

"It's code," says Daniel. "He knows that I know what he knows."

I laugh.

"You're writing now, aren't you?" Daniel says.

"How do you know?"

"You have a pen in your hand," says Daniel. "I'm almost as smart as Rex."

Surprisingly, Rex woofs.

"Hear that?" says Daniel. "He's talking to me."

"I hear," I say.

And Daniel and I sit there together, happy with Rex's company.

Daniel leaves to help tend his grandfather's sheep.

The L's come out in a while, peppy with sugar.

Rex waits patiently as they all pat him and go off. He will go back in and sit on his chair and wait for Lily to clear the dishes. For sure he will come up with a quote.

But inside, Lily is not clearing the dishes. She is sitting on the couch, crying.

"What's wrong?!" I ask.

Rex jumps up on the couch next to her.

"Nothing!" says Lily. "I love you, Rex!" She hugs Rex.

"The L's loved my story! They loved it."

Rex jumps off the couch and licks a plate, as if he knows she's happy and won't be clearing the dishes soon. He loves the left-over lemon cake. He ignores the cookies. Rex looks up at Lily.

"Go ahead, my friend. Finish the piece of cake left," says Lily.

And Rex does.

"I will send off my story to my editor," says Lily.

"What's the title of your story?" I ask Lily.

"*Messages*," says Lily, tears still on her cheeks.

"*Messages*," she repeats.

8.

THE STORY

Lily decides to go food shopping for the week.

"I have to buy food and snacks for my

dog!" she says. "*Our* dog," she adds. "And snacks for the L's."

"Get sugar snacks," I say, making Lily grin.

"Want to come?" she asks.

I shake my head. "Could I use your computer while you're gone? I'm practicing writing."

"Of course," says Lily. "Write away. I have a laptop computer I will give you when I get back."

When she leaves, it is quiet. Rex is sleeping in his dog bed.

It's just me. Alone.

I sit at the computer. I press the start button.

I hear Rex get up and stretch from leftover sleep. He comes over to look at me in Lily's chair. He gets up on his chair.

"I'm just practicing writing," I say to Rex. "I don't think you can help me."

Lily's desk is neat. There's no mess. There's no writers' help book titled *What Now?!*

I press the button that brings up a blank page.

"I have a title," I say to Rex. "But that's all I have."

I should feel odd talking to a dog, but I don't. Not to Rex.

I type the title.

A Bit of Magic.

"Those were Maxwell's words," I say to Rex. "About you. But now a blank page is all I have."

I sigh.

Then Rex reaches over and brings up a familiar quote.

If you find a book you really want to read but it hasn't been written yet, then you must write it.

—Toni Morrison

"I remember that," I say. "It was the very first quote you sent Lily. But I'm not a writer."

Rex sighs a dog sigh.

And then Rex does something new I've never seen.

He gently edges me from Lily's chair.

He sits in her chair and his paws move over the computer.

You are writing this book. Your story is about us.

I have goose bumps.

Rex jumps down and shakes his head at the door. I go over and open the door. Rex goes out.

I go back to the computer and stare at his words.

I reach over and print Rex's words on a

paper I can keep to read over and over.

I think about the secrets of writers.

"I'm a writer," Lily once said. "I believe most anything."

I believe most anything.

I am telling this story.

I am seven years old, and this is the story I've never read and must keep writing—in Toni Morrison's words—the story of a magic dog and a writer.

I'm a writer!

Another day my mother and father may learn Rex is magic—

Another day Maxwell will come visit with his trained chicken.

There will be more stories.

And I will write them.

9.
BOOK DREAMS

I have become a writer. It surprises me. It does not surprise my friend Daniel. Nothing surprises Daniel.

It does not surprise my teacher Ms. Luce, although when she reads the beginning of my story, "A Bit of Magic," it leaves her silent. After ten minutes she sits down, staring at me. She blows her nose. Is she crying?

"I can't believe your imagination, Grace!" she says.

I want to tell her I am living the story, that I am not really imaginative. She might be disappointed.

"And you're using your words!" she says.

An L once said in the writers' group, "If you're a writer, it's never over. You write and rewrite, and when you're finished you begin another story. An endless circle."

I never before understood what she might mean.

My parents come home from their medical conference sick with the flu. They are too sick to work. Too sick to eat. And they won't let me in the house. They don't want me to catch it.

"Pat Rex for me," my father says mournfully on the phone before he goes back to bed.

So I'm at Lily's.

She writes.

I stare at the laptop computer she has given me.

I need a new title. I need a quote, and a word or two or more.

I need an idea. Lily once told me it had to be *her* idea to write *her* story.

Lily can't tell me an idea that's right for me.

Rex doesn't know *my* ideas.

And then it happens.

It is teacher's meeting day at school. No

classes today. And the L's come to writers' group!

Rex greets them, and he sits in their group.

I become brave.

"Before I go to the dining room, where I can't hear you . . . ," I begin.

Lily smiles.

"I would like to know where your writing ideas come from."

Rex sits quietly, taking the snacks the L's offer. He listens.

They are happy to talk about book ideas. They're very peppy, even though they're eating apple slices, cheese, and carrots. No sugar.

"I am writing about my brave great-grandmother," says Laura.

"My childhood," says Lois.

"I'm writing about the future I want!" says Lana.

"I'm writing about a painting I have loved forever," says Lacy.

"My garden and the peace it brings me," says Lila.

"I'm writing about a birth," says Lou.

"About someone dying," says Laura.

"About love," says Lois.

"About the truths in magic," says Lily.

Rex and I look at each other. We know about that.

"About a dream," an L finishes.

A dream.

I suddenly remember something from when I was very little. Rex sees my expression.

"Thank you," I say to the L's.

"It was a good question, Grace," says Lois.

I leave them still talking about book ideas. I go to my laptop computer. I push the button for my title page—

A Bit of Magic

Rex jumps up on the chair beside me.

I delete the title "A Bit of Magic."

"You know I'm already writing that story," I say to Rex. "You're the one who told me."

Rex yawns as if pretending he doesn't remember that.

"I want to write about my dream when I was a little girl."

Rex looks at me oddly.

"I know, I know, I'm still a little girl,"
I say.

I type a new title on the blank page:

Book Dreams

"I wonder what you dream about," I say
to Rex, not expecting an answer.

Rex gently pushes me from my chair
and sits there. He writes:

I dream what I love.

"Me, too. What do you love, Rex?"
Rex writes.

Summer sun
Soft, silent snow
New bones
My work

And you.

I read his answer twice. It has the rhythm of dog poetry to me. I reach over and hug Rex and edge him off my chair.
I begin:

Book Dreams

When I was just a baby my mother and father read books to me . . .

10.

WORDS / NO WORDS

Lily and I take Rex to the vet for his check-up. We walk four blocks, carrying Rex's leash for when we're in the vet's office.

Rex sniffs noses with a small furry dog on her leash. We walk on, Rex smelling the sidewalk and lifting his leg by a tree.

"Sometimes I forget that Rex is a dog," I say.

"I know what you mean," says Lily.

We snap on the leash and open the door to the vet's office. Many assistants rush to us.

"Rex! One of our favorite dogs!"

Rex runs around in circles.

"Jake," calls one assistant. "Rex is here!"

Jake comes out of his office. Rex runs up to him, trailing his leash, and jumps up on Jake, the two of them face-to-face.

"Happy boy!" says Jake. He looks at us.

"No more sadness. You are great for him," he says.

"He's great for us, too," says Lily.

Jake examines Rex. "He's working for you?" he asks.

"He is," Lily and I say at the same time.

"What does he do?"

"He inspires me," says Lily.

"Us," I correct her.

"And he arranges the papers on my desk," says Lily.

Jake looks at her. He's silent. He opens the door to his inner office with his desk cluttered with papers.

"Not this bad, I hope," he says.

Rex goes in and begins arranging papers into neat piles. He picks up papers and a folder on the floor with his teeth, putting them neatly on the desk.

Then Rex sits.

"He only does that for people he likes," I say.

"I have no words for what I just saw," says Jake to us. "No words at all. And if I told you what I'm thinking, it would sound crazy."

"I know," says Lily. "I know."

Jake stares after us as we leave his office.

"Jake said 'no words,'" I say.

"We have all the words," says Lily.

"And Rex," I say.

We walk, Rex prancing, spreading happiness to everyone who stops to pat him.

Happiness all the way home.

We make applesauce for my sick mother and father. Daniel and Rex come with me to deliver it.

I knock.

My father answers the door.

"Are you growing a beard?" I ask.

I've never seen my father with a dark beard before.

Daniel smiles.

"I'm too sick to shave," says my father. He takes the big bowl of applesauce. Lily has put a design of thin-sliced apple rounds on the top.

"Hello, Daniel," says my father.

"I'm sorry you're sick," says Daniel.

"Me, too. Hello, Rex," my father says, with more expression.

He takes an apple slice off the top of the applesauce and hands it to Rex. Rex loves apple slices, and he eats it and woofs.

"I have to lie down," says my father. He closes the door. Our visit is over.

"He looks really sick," says Daniel as we walk back to Lily's. "I never thought about doctors getting sick. That's not normal."

I laugh.

We sit on the steps.

"How's it going?" asks Daniel.

"What?"

"You know what," says Daniel. "I have Ms. Luce's assignment written out for us. In case you've forgotten."

"I haven't forgotten," I say.

He takes it out of his pocket and reads it.

"'Write a short essay, story, poem, or observation about what you love. Use your words!' Did you write about what you love?"

"I began it," I say.

"What's it called?"

"'Book Dreams.' What did you write?"

"A kind of poem," says Daniel.

I smile. "Do you have a title?" I ask.

"'Walking over Sheep,'" says Daniel, grinning at me.

Rex woofs.

"Rex likes my title," says Daniel.

"Rex likes words," I say.

Then Lily opens the door to give us a plate of thin-sliced apples that we share with Rex.

11.

SURPRISES

It's raining when I go to my house to get clean clothes to wear. My parents have warned me to go right to my room and stay away from them.

Rex comes with me, a surprise because he does not list rain on the things he loves.

My father opens the door and we go in.

"Rex, you came, too," my father says. "I have snacks for you."

My father opens a bag of dog snacks and gives Rex two. Rex is happy.

I go to my room and gather clean clothes.

When I come out Rex is in my mother and father's bedroom, clothes scattered around. My mother waves from her bed.

"What is Rex doing?" asks my father suddenly.

A second surprise.

Rex is not acting like a "regular" dog today. He is gathering the clothes from around the room and putting them in the laundry basket.

My father stares.

I remember what I said to Jake the vet

when Rex arranged Jake's desk papers.

"He only does that for people he likes," I had said.

My father sits on his bed and watches.

"Amazing," says my father.

Rex finishes by picking up magazines on the floor and putting them on my father's bed in a neat pile.

"I'm going now," I say. "I hope you feel better."

Rex and I leave my parents' bedroom.

"Amazing," I hear my father say again before we go out the door.

The rain begins to fall harder.

I gather the clothes in my jacket, and we run.

"Snacks, right?" I say to Rex. "You cleaned up for my parents because you wanted more snacks. And, surprise, I think you *like* them!"

Rex looks at me innocently.

We run home as the rain comes down hard.

Lily smiles when I tell her Rex cleaned up my parents' bedroom.

"Your father has always liked Rex," she

says. "Rex knows that."

"And Father gave Rex snacks," I say.

"The L's feed him snacks," Lily says. "And he'll never let them know he has magical powers."

"True."

"I think your father won't think of Rex as 'magical,'" says Lily. "Just very talented. And I know one thing about Rex that you may not know yet."

"What?"

"Rex is kind and smart and magical. He has humor."

"Yes."

"But Rex is also sly."

I look closely at Rex.

"Sly?" I ask. "Like sneaky?"

"I think of it as a sneaky truth with a bit of humor," says Lily.

Rex yawns, then gives me a new look. He goes over to the computer. He pushes the button for a blank page. He writes:

I like to surprise people.

Sly. With a little humor.

12.

A "WONDROUS" THING

Things are happening all at once.

School will be over in a few months.

I will turn eight years old in the summer.

My parents are better and are back at work. They look at Rex in a different way now, especially my father. The word "amazing" is an everyday word for Rex.

"My life is getting big," I say to Lily.

"I think you mean 'full,'" says Lily.

"Maybe I don't want it full," I say. "Maybe I want it to stay the same."

Lily looks at me for a moment.

"Nothing stays the same forever, Grace," she says. "It changes in ways that only you will know."

"I don't like that, Lily."

"I know, Gracie. I know."

Rex continues to be Rex, though I now know he is sly as well as smart and kind, and magical.

I also know that things will change.

On the last day of school there is a picnic to celebrate. Lily and my parents are there, and

Rex, who plays with other dogs in the park.

Ms. Luce pins all our writing on a large bulletin board.

Book Dreams

When I was just a baby my mother and father read books to me.

I loved books, the smell of them, the smooth, bright pages that I loved turning.

And the words.

In my crib one night my mother and father found me turning pages in my sleep.

I had book dreams then.

I have book dreams now.

—*Grace*

When my mother and father read "Book Dreams," they get tears in their eyes, remembering.

I read Daniel's "kind of" poem, as he puts it.

Running over Sheep

My white dog runs over the flock of sheep—
White over white
Cloud over cloud—
A small, fierce, loyal protector.

—Daniel

"I like this," I say to Daniel. "'Cloud over cloud.'"

"Thank you," says Daniel. He thinks for a moment.

"I always knew you were a writer, Grace," he says, almost in a whisper.

I look to see if he's joking. He isn't.

"Maybe you're a writer, too," I say.

He smiles and shakes his head.

"I'd rather run over a flock of sheep," he says.

My parents drive us all home before they head off to work, Rex with his muzzle out the window, ears flying back.

"There's a man with a tall hat walking up to your door," my father says to Lily as he stops.

"That's my friend Maxwell," says Lily, getting out of the car.

"Does he have a chicken in his arms?" asks my mother.

"It's probably not real," I say.

My words startle me. I don't want to say where Rex began and why he's with Lily now.

"Are you sure?" my mother asks.

My life is full of half-truths and secrets these days, I think. *Maybe* I'm *sly like Rex.*

We wave goodbye.

It is Maxwell carrying a live bright-red-and-orange chicken.

He stops to pat Rex.

"Come in, come in," says Lily. "And this is?" she continues, stroking the chicken.

"It is Lucy-Lou, my hen," says Maxwell. "I didn't name her," he adds.

"I hope not," says Lily. "Can't you just call her Lucy?"

"I do," says Maxwell. "Bow, Lucy."

Lucy bows her head to us and eats corn from Maxwell's hand.

"Bark to the dog, Lucy," he says.

Lucy opens her beak and makes three short squawks at Rex.

Rex barks back.

And Lucy shows us she can count—"one squawk, two squawks, three squawks"—and on.

"She's affectionate," says Maxwell.

He hands her to me, and she nestles in my arms. She is warm.

"I've never held a chicken before," I say.

Lucy is quiet.

"Never," I add with a smile at Maxwell. "This is a wondrous happening."

"Ah yes, wondrous! I can't begin to count all the new and wondrous things that will happen to you," says Maxwell. "And you will know what to do with them. Keep that like a whisper in your head."

Maxwell pretends to whisper in my ear. Lucy lays her head against me. And I think of his words.

He has given us Rex. Rex is a wondrous thing.

Can there possibly be any other wondrous thing?

It is evening, and my parents are working late.

Tomorrow the L's come to writers' group again.

Rex will sit in their group. He will listen and every so often push the glass doors open for me so I hear more clearly.

I think about Maxwell's words to me. They sounded like a promise. I also remember Lily saying things don't stay the same. But things will change in ways only I will know.

I go to my laptop computer and press the key for a blank page. I write:

Wondrous Things

Rex comes into the dining room and watches.

"Blank screen," I say to Rex.

Rex does what I secretly hope he will do. He nudges me off the chair.

He sits and writes:

You know. The whisper.

I know?

Rex gets down and goes into the kitchen to drink water. I know? What is it Rex knows that I know?

I think of Maxwell's words.

And I suddenly know what it is I know!

I write:

> *I am seven years old.*
> *I am a writer.*
> *But I know things don't stay the same.*
> *I know a wondrous thing.*
> *When I am grown, I will not have Rex.*
> *But so that doesn't make me sad*
> *I will have*
> *a whisper in my head—*
> *who finds me quotes—*
> *who sends words that untangle*
> *and shape a story—*
> *I will name that whisper "Rex."*
>   *—Grace*

I go to bed. I know that Rex will come.

And he does. He lies next to me and puts
his front leg around me. Like a hug.

A wondrous thing.